For Ruth and her tree

Visit An's website at www.vrombaut.co.uk

OXFORD
UNIVERSITY PRESS

Great Clarendon Street, Oxford OX2 6DP

Oxford University Press is a department of the University of Oxford.
It furthers the University's objective of excellence in research, scholarship,
and education by publishing worldwide in

Oxford   New York

Auckland Bangkok Buenos Aires Cape Town Chennai Dar es Salaam Delhi
Hong Kong Istanbul Karachi Kolkata Kuala Lumpur Madrid Melbourne Mexico City
Mumbai Nairobi São Paulo Shanghai Taipei Tokyo Toronto

Oxford is a registered trade mark of Oxford University Press in the UK and in certain other countries

Text and Illustrations © An Vrombaut 2004

The moral rights of the author/artist have been asserted

Database right Oxford University Press (maker)

First published 2004

British Library Cataloguing in Publication Data available

ISBN 0-19-279142-7 (hardback)
ISBN 0-19-272575-0 (paperback)

10 9 8 7 6 5 4 3 2 1

Printed in Thailand

The Lost Acorns

An Vrombaut

OXFORD

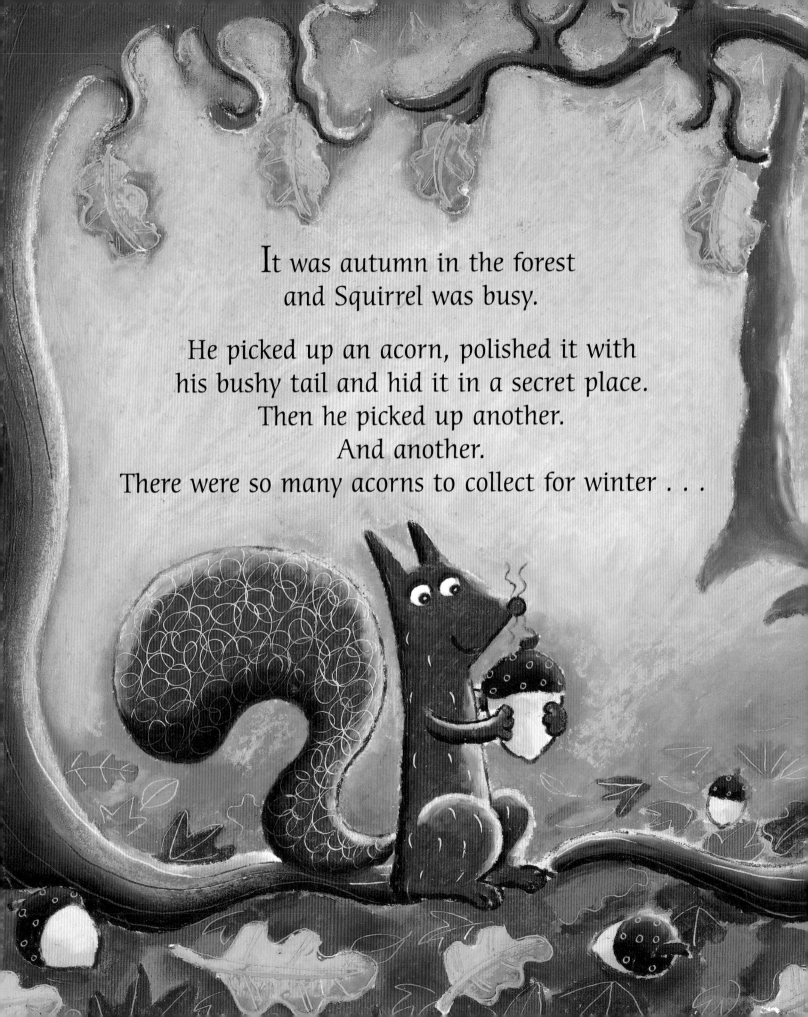

It was autumn in the forest
and Squirrel was busy.

He picked up an acorn, polished it with
his bushy tail and hid it in a secret place.
Then he picked up another.
And another.
There were so many acorns to collect for winter . . .

And so many acorn hiding
places for Squirrel to remember.

By the winding path,
beneath the silver birches.

Under the pink pebble
on the riverbank.

In the hollow log beside
the mossy tree stump.

Between the tangled roots
of the old beech tree.
Or was it the old
chestnut *tree?*

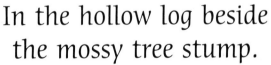

Squirrel tried hard to remember,
but a fuzzy feeling came into his head.
It was no use. He'd forgotten.

'Oh dear,' he sighed.
And then he had a brilliant idea.
'I'll hide all the acorns TOGETHER!
Then I'll only need to remember
ONE hiding place!'

So Squirrel dug a big hole,

and rolled all his acorns into it.

He covered them with soil,

and raked it with a twig.

And finally he marked the spot
with a long knobbly stick,
a bright red maple leaf,
and the plumpest mushroom in the forest.
'Perfect!' said Squirrel and went home for a rest.
Meanwhile . . .

Toad was looking for a
comfy chair for his burrow.
He tried some mushrooms.

One was too **wobbly**.

One was too
squishy.

One was too
spotty.

Then Toad saw the **plumpest** mushroom in the forest.

'Perfect!' he croaked with a broad toad smile.

Mouse hurried home in the rain.

'If only I had an umbrella . . .'
she sighed.

Then she saw
a bright red
maple leaf.

'Perfect!' she squeaked
with a little mouse giggle.

Bat was in his cave. He had a **problem**.
'These walls are too slippery,' he thought.
'I need something to hold on to.'
Then he saw a long, knobbly stick.

'Perfect!' he grinned
with a cheerful
bat chuckle.

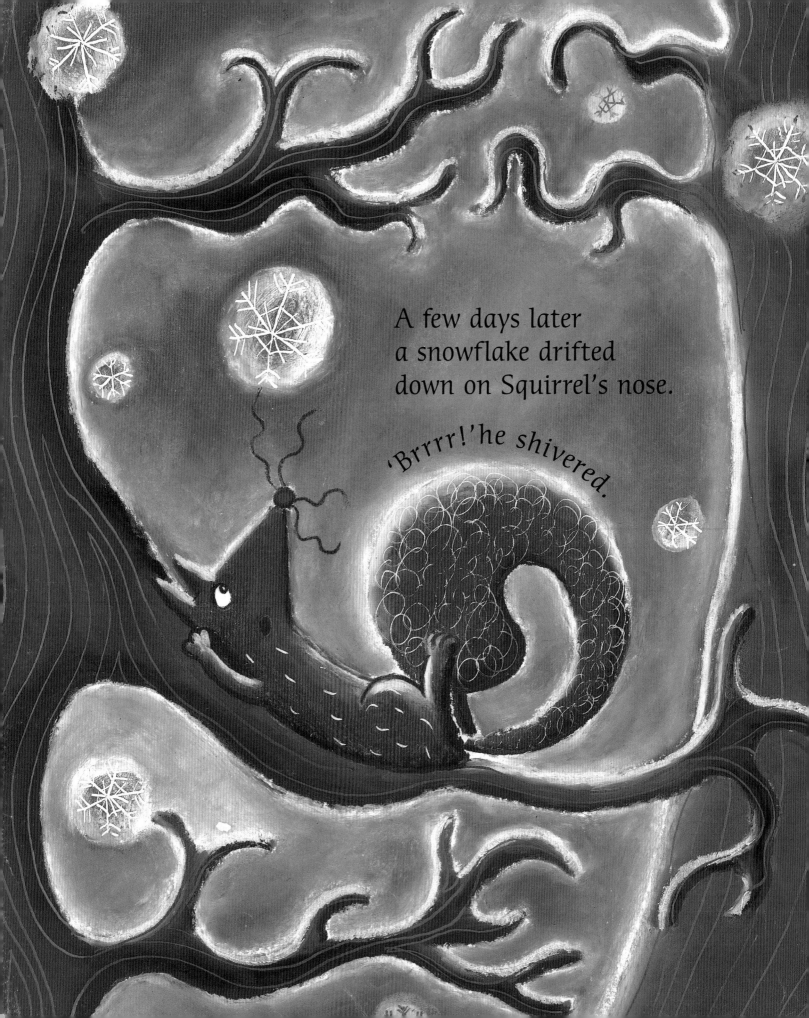

A few days later
a snowflake drifted
down on Squirrel's nose.

'Brrrr!' he shivered.

'It must be winter. Time to check on my acorn treasure!'

He searched and searched.

But he couldn't find it anywhere.

Then he had another brilliant idea.

He could ask Toad, Mouse, and Bat for help.

'Have you seen a long knobbly stick
and a bright red maple leaf and the
plumpest mushroom in the forest?' asked Squirrel.

Toad, Mouse, and Bat blushed.

'Sorry,' they said.
'We didn't know these were yours.'

'Thank you,' said Squirrel. 'But what I'm *really* looking for is my acorn treasure. Now I've lost it forever and I'll have nothing to eat all winter.'

'Don't worry,' said Toad, Mouse, and Bat. 'We'll help you.'

And so all through the long cold winter, Bat fed Squirrel upside-down breakfasts.

Crunchy grasshoppers with milk. 'Yummy!' said Squirrel.

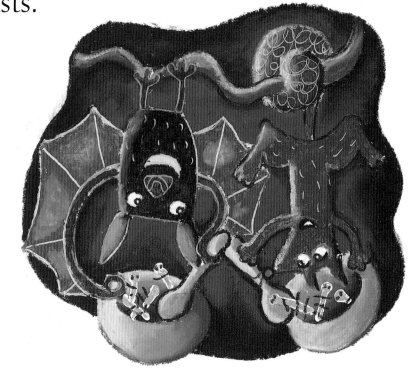

Mouse invited Squirrel for lazy lunches.

Baked turnip with corn, and blackberries for dessert. 'Very nice!' said Squirrel.

And Toad served Squirrel scrumptious suppers.

Pondweed soup
and worm
spaghetti.
'More please!'
said Squirrel.

Squirrel enjoyed all the delicious food his
friends made for him.

But sometimes
he wondered what
had happened to
his lost acorns.

At last it was spring.
Toad, Mouse, and Bat came out of their houses.

'Where's Squirrel?' they asked.

They knocked on his tree but he wasn't at home.
So they strolled through the forest,
looking at the grass and smelling the flowers . . .

And then they saw him,
standing in a circle of
green oak leaves.

'I've found my acorns!' Squirrel smiled.
'And look how they've grown!'